DAGMAR SCHULTZ
AND THE
POWERS OF
DARKNESS

DAGMAR SCHULTZ
AND THE
POWERS OF
DARKNESS

LYNN HALL

ALADDIN BOOKS

Macmillan Publishing Company   New York

Maxwell Macmillan Canada   Toronto

Maxwell Macmillan International
New York   Oxford   Singapore   Sydney

First Aladdin Books edition 1992

Aladdin Books
Macmillan Publishing Company
866 Third Avenue
New York, NY 10022

Maxwell Macmillan Canada
1200 Eglinton Avenue East
Suite 200
Don Mills, Ontario M3C 3N1

Macmillan Publishing Company is part of the Maxwell Communication Group of Companies.

Printed in the United States of America
A hardcover edition of *Dagmar Schultz and the Powers of Darkness* is available from Charles Scribner's Sons, Macmillan Publishing Company.

10 9 8 7 6 5 4 3 2 1

Library of Congress Cataloging-in-Publication Data
Hall, Lynn.
    Dagmar Schultz and the powers of darkness / Lynn Hall.
        p.   cm.
    Summary: Dagmar makes a deal with Edgar, the only warlock in New Berlin, Iowa: She will convince Aunt Gretchen to go out with him if he will use his powers to make James Mann fall in love with her.
    ISBN 0-689-71547-1
    [1. Witches—Fiction.   2. Humorous stories.   3. Iowa—Fiction.]
I. Title.
PZ7.H1458Dah   1992
[Fic]—dc20   91-27939

DAGMAR SCHULTZ AND THE POWERS OF DARKNESS

One

I do some pretty stupid things sometimes. Usually it's because I don't know any better, but some of the time I do know better and just can't stop myself.

Like walking past James Mann's house. I know better. I know he won't magically look up and see me walking past and fall in love with me, or even speak to me. But still I keep doing it. I keep thinking, if I walk past his house something good *might* happen, and if I don't there's no possibility at all.

You're probably thinking I'm some kind of pathetic, scruffy slob, having to chase a boy that way, but I'm not. I'm going to be a knockout in a few years, as soon as everything is in place. Right now I'm only actually beautiful in the hair department. My hair is very long and thick. I can't sit on it yet without breaking my neck, but I can hide in it when I need to. And it's very sexy.

In just roughly twenty-nine days I'm going to be thirteen, and I expect a gorgeous figure to start popping out as soon as I hit the big One-Three. So of course I've been working on getting boyfriends lined up. Mom has promised me a set of false fingernails for my birthday, and I don't want them to go to waste without a boyfriend to admire them.

The trouble is, I live in New Berlin, Iowa. Pronounced like Merlin. Three hundred and fifty population, and none of them interesting boys.

Of course there are boys at school, and I've got my eye peeled at all times, painful though it may sound. But the best bet I've been able to come up with is James Mann, for several reasons. One, he rides the same bus I do and lives right down the road from my cousin Neese, so I have an excuse to be walking out his road. Two, he's gorgeous. Three, he doesn't already have a girlfriend.

I say he's gorgeous, but everybody might not agree with that, I suppose. He's thirteen, he's tall and slim, and has longish light brown hair and sort of sensitive lips. If you know what I mean. And his eyes. When you look in his eyes you can see that he has suffered. I don't know what from. I only looked in his eyes once, when I had my timing down absolutely perfect and ran into him getting onto the bus. I'd tried for three weeks to time it that way.

One other thing you should know about James. He

2

is an heir. He's the oldest son of an oldest son of an oldest son. That means he's going to inherit a big, beautiful farm that's been paid for for fifty years, with a big limestone house and one of the best dairy set-ups in the county. Everyone says whoever marries James Mann is going to fall into a pot of honey.

Naturally any guy in that position is going to be hard to get. He'll never need to chase a girl in his whole life. He can just sit back and take applications.

Unless I win his heart and become his unforgettable first love.

So that was why I was standing in the road in front of my cousin Neese's house at four o'clock on Wednesday afternoon, trying not to look like I was lining up to have a run at James Mann. Which of course I was. And Neese is nobody's fool, even if she does have awful fat hips and frizzy hair.

She's in high school, so she rides a different bus, but she was out there in the road when I got off my bus. She was leaning on the mailbox, going through the catalogs and junk that had come in the mail.

Uncle Dean and Aunt Dorothy have a place almost as good as the Manns'. It's got a big stone house, too, and nice barns and pretty windbreak pines along the north and west sides of the buildings. Out close to the road is a sign that says Kountry Kut and Kurl. That's Aunt Dorothy's beauty shop, around at the side door.

Neese looked up at me as the bus drove away. "You again," she said without much interest. She'd

3

found a fashion catalog and was looking at hand-knit Shetland sweaters imported from Scotland, where they were knitted in cottages. She showed me the page.

"What are you doing out here, ho-ho, as if I didn't know," she said, still looking through the catalog.

"Oh, nothing," I said casually. "I just felt like a walk. The trees are so pretty, this time of year."

It was pretty along that road in October, with the hayfields bright green still and the woods turning red and gold and the far hills looking blue and purple. But of course that wasn't why I was there.

Neese snorted and shot me a look, like "Who do you think you're kidding?" I got a little red but held my ground.

"He's not going to notice you," she said flatly. "He's into basketball this year."

"I don't know who you're talking about. And besides, I might go out for cheerleading. He'd notice me if I was a cheerleader."

She bundled all the mail into her chubby arms and started up the lane toward her house. "Don't hold your breath, Dagmar. You've got a long way to go before you start looking more interesting than a basketball."

"Thanks for all your wonderful support," I yelled after her, and turned to walk the two miles back toward town feeling like a deflated fool.

It was a tan gravel road with interesting things growing in the ditches, wild asparagus and Queen

4

Anne's lace and wild raspberries and some dark purple flowers I didn't know the name of. And it was a beautiful sunny fall afternoon. If I really had been walking that road just to enjoy nature, I'd have enjoyed nature.

But I had a mission: to win the heart of the elusive James. Mission impossible.

His house was on the left side of the road. It had a sign by its mailbox, too, a cow-shaped sign painted like a holstein. It said High View Acres. In farm-shop class, the kids make signs like that and get semester credits for them. I thought James's sign was one of the best I'd ever seen.

He was out there!

He was shooting baskets to a hoop on the front of the machine shed, and he was all alone. I slowed up as much as I could and tried not to look obviously obvious.

Their Australian shepherd came running out and barked his fool head off at me, so I stopped and patted my legs till he shut up and came over to get petted. I knew James knew I was there. When your dog barks, you look.

Slowly I raised my head for a casual glance in his direction. He was crouching for a free throw. It missed.

"Nice try," I called. If I'd just walked past without saying anything, the whole two-mile walk would have been wasted.

He turned and looked at me. Didn't say anything.

"I was just over at Neese's," I explained loudly.

He grunted something and lined up for another shot.

Stone-cold dead in the water, I told myself as I gave the dog a final pat and turned to head home. You are stone-cold dead in the water, Dagmar Schultz. He is never going to notice you. Give up on him and quit breaking your heart.

But I couldn't. I could only hide in my hair and plod on home.

TWO

Our house is kind of a big old place that used to be fancy. One side is turquoise, two sides are tan with brown trim, and the back is dirty white. My dad never seems to stay with a house-painting mood past one side of the house.

You'd like my dad. He's kind of old for a dad, but he's funny. He looks stringy and leathery and tough; at least he looks tough when he isn't popping his upper false teeth out of his mouth to make the little kids laugh.

We have lots of little kids in our family. I'm the oldest—and best, of course. Then there's my brother Cootie, who is fairly rotten, my sister GeorgeAnn— nobody can stand her—then David and Deaney, who aren't too bad, and the baby, Delight, who isn't much of anything yet.

As soon as I got home I did my homework, thinking I might go into town after supper and watch bowling, since it was Wednesday night. My aunt Gretchen bowls in a mixed league on Wednesday nights, and usually Dad or Mom or both, or all of us, go in and watch awhile, just for something to do.

That night after supper and dishes, Daddy said, "I guess I'll go in and watch bowling for a while. Anybody want to come?"

Mom thought about it but decided not to. She's very big, and usually by the end of the day she's worn-out from taking care of us kids and playing with Delight and carrying all her weight around.

GeorgeAnn said she wanted to go, but Mom said, "You better stay home and get your practicing done, little sister." GeorgeAnn was going to play "Twinkling Stars" and "Over the Waves" at a piano recital in two weeks. I thought it was brave and motherly of Mom to volunteer to spend the evening listening to those two songs over and over and *over*.

David and Deaney were too little to be much interested, so it was just Cootie and Daddy and I who drove to Strawberry Point in the pickup.

The Berry Bowl is one of my favorite places. It's so noisy in there, with balls rumbling down the alleys and pins clattering all over the place, and people yelling and laughing back and forth. It isn't a very big bowling alley, only six lanes, but it's nice and friendly and exciting.

You'd like my aunt Gretchen. Probably. Maybe. Well, I like her, when she isn't grabbing me by the hair and pulling me over backward, or jabbing me in the gut. She is Mom's sister, but it's Daddy who's her real buddy.

Aunt Gretchen is a bookkeeper for the Happy Auto Body Shop. She's paid more than any other bookkeeper in town just because she pitches for their softball team, which is always in the regional finals. She also is the star bowler on the Happy Bodies team in the town league.

She was sitting on the curved bench with her team when we came in.

"Earl the Pearl," she bellowed, and grabbed Daddy by the nape of the neck and shook him till his eyeballs rolled.

"Say there, Hair," she said to me, and made a grab for my hair over the back of the bench. I was too quick for her. Cootie had already slipped off someplace with some kids he knew. We'd only get fleeting glimpses of him for the rest of the night, which was fine with me.

"How you doing?" Daddy asked, peering toward the scoresheet.

"Ahg," Aunt Gretchen snarled, "we're a little behind, but we just got started. Just a little behind," she hooted, reaching around to pat Daddy's butt.

It was her turn to bowl then. She got up, sucked in a lungful of smoky air, jammed her shirttail in with her thumbs, and strode forward, her custom-made black-and-red ball balanced like treasure on her fingertips.

She snapped her heels together, stood as tall and

straight as a chunky, busty woman can, and closed her eyes for a moment of silent prayer or whatever it was that she always did just before she let go.

Then, the dipping step, the backswing, three little fast steps, and the throw! She crouched there with one leg crossed clear over, practically on the floor, while the ball curved toward the gutter. We all held our breaths. It straightened just in the nick of time, skimming the rim of the gutter before it curved into the pocket and blew all ten pins right off the map.

When the yelling and back thumping were over, I got some money from Daddy and left to wander up and down the alleys looking for interesting people. I didn't find any, so I settled down at one of the little tables between the alleys and the bar, with a Coke and a bag of sour-cream-and-onion-flavored Ripple Chips. You have to be careful of those little tables. They have just one leg, up the middle, and if you try to sit on them they fall over.

I sat there crunching and wishing I'd brought Shelly along for company. She's not too crazy about the bowling alley, but she'd have come if I'd asked her. We could have sat there looking young and beautiful, chattering away, and some incredibly terrific guy would come in. No, two guys, one terrific one for me and one average one for Shelly.

They'd come over and pull up a couple of empty chairs and start talking and flirting, and we'd talk and flirt back, and they'd offer to drive us home and Daddy would say okay, and on the way home the terrific one would pick up my hand and hold it. He'd be driving, of course. He'd have to be the one who had the car, otherwise Shelly would be getting the better one. He'd pick up my hand and gaze into my eyes. Then he'd raise my hand to his lips and put little kisses on each finger. And then he'd say . . .

Somebody bowled another strike and the noise of the yelling broke me out of my daydream. From where I sat it looked like Aunt Gretchen had done it. While my eyes were turned in that direction I noticed a man sitting at a table like mine and staring at Aunt Gretchen. He was down at the end of the room where the light wasn't very bright. Probably he'd been sitting there the whole time and I hadn't seen him, since he wasn't what I was looking for.

He was the kind of man you'd never see, even if he'd been in the lighted end of the room. He was old, maybe thirty or forty, and sort of colorless and scrawny-looking. His hair had receded at the top corners of his face till it was almost out of sight, but with a hunk left in the center, like a horse's forelock. And his glasses were so round and thick that they looked like bottle bottoms.

But what made me notice him was the way he just sat there and stared at Aunt Gretchen. It was like he'd never seen anybody bowl a strike before.

Oh, well, the world was full of strange people. No skin off my nose if he wanted to stare at my aunt. I went back into my daydream. Shelly wasn't with me this time. Just me sitting here eating potato chips when this incredibly gorgeous guy comes up to the table and says . . .

"Do you care if I sit here?"

It was a real voice, and it about jolted me out of my drawers. I choked on my potato chip and looked up.

Rats. Not the gorgeous guy of my dreams. Only the creep who had been watching Aunt Gretchen.

"There's plenty of empty tables," I said rather rudely. I didn't want him to think he could just walk up and start talking to me when I didn't even know him.

But he sat down anyway, and smiled a kind of sweet smile at me. "I'm sorry to intrude," he said.

Nobody I know would ever say "I'm sorry to intrude."

"That's okay," I said grudgingly.

He motioned with his head toward Aunt Gretchen and said, "You know that lady over there, the one who just bowled?"

"Aunt Gretchen," I said, digging out the last little broken chip and savoring it on my tongue.

"She's your aunt? I saw you talking to her, but I didn't know you were related." His eyes lit up, although it was hard to tell because his glasses were so thick his eyes looked teeny and kept moving from side to side when he moved his head. They didn't really move, of course. It was just the curve of those thick glasses that gave that impression.

I nodded. "So?"

He didn't answer. He looked like he was off on a daydream like the one I'd just been on. After a minute he snapped out of it and focused his eyes squarely on me.

"Let me introduce myself," he said, and held out a hand. "Edgar Temple, assistant meat manager at the A & P."

I wiped the potato chip grease from my hand onto my jeans and shook with him. "Dagmar Schultz. Student."

He looked at me for a minute as if he was sizing me up or coming to a decision. Finally he said, "Tell me, Dagmar, if you could have your heart's desire, what would it be?"

"James Mann falling in love with me," I said. I didn't even need to think about that one.

He smiled. He had little, short, square teeth, very white and straight, just like Daddy's false ones.

"I could make that wish come true for you," he said softly.

I gave him a fishy look. "Go on," I scoffed.

"Yes. It's true. I could." He leaned across the table and whispered, "I'm not only an assistant meat manager. I'm also a witch."

Three

I stared at him. "Get out of here," I snorted.

"No, really. I am a witch. Well, warlock if you want the technical term. Women are witches, men are warlocks. But it's the same thing."

I was beginning to see what Mom and Daddy meant when they warned me about talking to strange men. I'd never met a stranger one than this. Still, I didn't figure he could kidnap me or do anything horrible to me, right here in the Berry Bowl Café and Bowling Alley, with Daddy and Aunt Gretchen a few yards away and Cootie chasing Kevin Borcard around the tables.

"You couldn't be a witch," I challenged the guy. "Witches don't live in Strawberry Point, Iowa. Only normal people live here."

"You think I'm not a normal person?" His glasses flashed and made his eyes jump around behind them, and his voice went up into a kind of squeak. "You think I don't have the same wants and needs as anybody else? You think I don't bleed when I cut myself?"

He was getting a little hostile. Daddy turned around and looked over at me to make sure I was okay when Edgar's voice climbed to that last note.

"Well, you just told me you're a witch. What do you expect? Either you're a witch or you're a normal person. You can't have it both ways."

He simmered down a little and kind of slumped onto his elbows. I held out the potato chip bag, remembered it was empty, and just gave him a sympathetic shrug.

In a calmer voice he went on, "It might surprise you to know that there are witches everywhere, even in Strawberry Point, Iowa. Not very many, though. That's our big problem around here; we keep losing our covens."

"Okay." I sighed. "I'll play your silly game. What is a coven?"

He looked at me, trying to decide whether I was putting him on or not. "A coven is thirteen witches. You have to have thirteen in order to have an active coven, and we can never seem to get more than six or seven. Nobody wants to drive very far, especially in winter, and if our meetings conflict with something good on television, nobody shows up. Sometimes Mother and I have been the only ones who showed up for a meeting, and you know you can't run a coven that way."

I nodded in agreement. I was a little dazed by all this, but fascinated. "Your mother is a witch, too?"

"Oh yes. Certainly. It's pretty much an inherited gift, you know. Mother was the best we had in Strawberry Coven. You should have seen the way she could change price markers in K Mart. Well, any store, for that matter, although of course she never did it in my store. At least, I never caught her. . . ." His voice faded thoughtfully.

"Changed price markers?" I leaned across the table toward him, thoroughly hooked. "Your mother could change prices on things in stores? Wow."

"Oh yes. We didn't pay retail for anything for years. And she could make people sneeze or yawn, that was one of her favorite ones. If we were driving and pulled up to a four-way stop, she could keep all the other drivers sneezing so hard they couldn't drive, and we'd sail right through. She was really quite talented. But . . ."

He looked sad and quit talking.

"Did she die?" I asked sympathetically.

He shook his head. "Worse than that. She became a Lutheran. She started driving our neighbor lady to church after the woman's husband died. Mother had always dreamed about singing in public; not that her voice was any good, you know, but it was her dream. Well, she got hooked on the idea of singing in the

Lutheran church choir, wearing the blue robe with the gold satin collar and all that. And of course you can't really be a practicing Lutheran and a practicing witch at the same time. It's frowned upon by both organizations."

"So your mom gave up witching?"

He drooped some more and nodded his head. We sat in sad silence for a minute. Then, with sudden determination, he turned his eyes full force on me and said, "You have to help me."

I stared at him blankly, then shoved my chair way back. "Oh no. Forget it, turkey. You're not getting me to join any coven. I didn't even join 4-H. I'm a practicing Methodist. You're barking up the wrong girl here, buster."

"No, no." He flapped his hands between us, agitated. "That's not what I want from you. Gracious. You're not witch material. Anybody could see that."

I wasn't so sure I liked that.

"Besides," he said, "you don't go around picking up converts in a bowling alley. People have the gift or they don't. No, what I want from you is a very simple favor, and in exchange I'm willing to put all my powers at your disposal, toward whatever end you wish. Does that sound fair?"

"It sounds totally off-the-wall. If you'll pardon my saying so, Edgar, I think you're missing some spots from your dice. I don't think all your pistons are firing. You're out of your tree. You are a total nut sundae. No offense."

"None taken." He sighed. "That's what most people think when I tell them I'm a . . . you know. So you can understand why I don't mention it unless I have to, and I trust that you'll respect my confidence and keep your lip zipped about this."

I more or less nodded.

"Good. I knew I could trust you. Now, back to business. All I want you to do is to get your aunt Gretchen to go out with me."

My jaw dropped a foot. My eyes bugged out. I didn't want to laugh at him and hurt his feelings, but the biggest wave of laughter I have ever felt in my life just swamped me. I roared. I almost fell over backward in my chair. Then I realized people were frowning at me, Daddy especially. I guess even a bowling alley has its noise limits.

Edgar was waiting with tightly pressed lips. He didn't have much in the way of lips to begin with, and wearing that expression, they disappeared completely.

"I'm sorry," I said, blowing my nose and forcing my face straight. "I didn't mean to laugh like that. I wasn't laughing *at* you, Edgar, I was laughing *with* you."

"But I'm not laughing," he said, dead serious, and I sputtered again, trying to fight it down.

"Okay, now," I said finally. "Okay, here we go. I'm all through laughing now. Tell me why you want to go out with . . ." I couldn't finish the sentence. I had to clamp down on the laugh urge too hard.

"I've fallen in love with her," he said simply, and that sobered me up right away. I know from my own bitter experience with James, love is nothing to laugh about.

All I could think of to say to him was, "Why?"

Edgar looked down at the table and said in a low voice, "I don't expect anyone of your tender years to understand this, but life can be very lonely for a bachelor, especially in a town like this. And I want children. I need children to pass my powers on to, the way Mother passed them to me. We can't let these wondrous powers die, can we? And they will die, if I don't marry and have children."

"No, we wouldn't want that," I said faintly, thinking about altering price markers in K Mart and making people sneeze at stop signs.

"I've been coming to the bowling alley for weeks now, just to watch Gretchen," he said. I could tell from the way he said "Gretchen" that he really was in love with her. It was the same way I said "James" to myself.

"I've tried talking to her, offering to buy her a beer after her game, things like that," Edgar said wistfully. "But she's always busy."

I could imagine what her exact words must have been. "Buzz off, pip-squeak" would be the politest guess I'd make.

This whole thing was beginning to fascinate me. "So, let me get this straight. I fix you up with Aunt Gretchen, and in exchange, you use your powers to get me James?"

His eyes hit mine with all their intensity, and for the first time I really believed he was a witch. "Yes."

"Wait a minute, here. If you have the power to make James fall in love with me, why don't you just use it on Aunt Gretchen, directly, instead of going all around the hog house?"

"I've tried," he said, almost weeping. "Don't you think I've tried? I aimed everything I had at her, and the most I got was blowing the breaker switches on the electrical system and plunging the whole place into five minutes of darkness. It often works that way, when you try to use your powers for direct personal gain."

"You don't call stealing from K Mart direct personal gain?"

"Not on the same level as bending a powerful woman like Gretchen to my will, it isn't. A young boy like your James, he won't be any trouble at all. It's just that Gretchen is such a strong force herself. That's why I love her so much. It's why I want her to bear my children."

I thought about it all through the new Coke and bag of potato chips Edgar bought me as a bribe. Finally I leaned the chair back on its hind legs and said, "Okay, Edgar, you're on. What have I got to lose?"

Four

It was ten o'clock before we started home. Cootie was singing loudly, the way he does when he's fighting sleepiness. I, of course, was not fighting sleepiness. I was wired with excitement.

It was still hard to believe there were real live witches in Strawberry Point, Iowa, but the more I thought about it, the more believable it became. After all, look at the men going by on the sidewalk. You can't tell which one belongs to Knights of Columbus, or the Benevolent Paternal Order of Elks, or the Masonic Lodge. How would you know who belongs to the Strawberry Point witch coven? I mean, everybody knows they don't fly around on brooms, wearing pointy hats and warts on their chins.

Although, of course, Edgar's mother could have warts on her chin, for all I knew.

21

Aunt Gretchen had to drive two of her team members home, but before we got to the edge of New Berlin her headlights were in our rearview mirror. She pulled her huge old Chrysler into our driveway and clumped up behind us to the house, grabbing at my hair.

I wanted to stay up and listen in while they talked, but Mom said the dread words "school night" and chased Cootie and me up the stairs.

I hid at the top in the linen closet till Cootie was done in the bathroom and safe in his room with the door shut. Then I snuck back down the stairs just far enough to hear them talking. The three of them were in the living room watching the sports part of the news.

As soon as it was over, Aunt Gretchen got up out of her chair and turned off the TV.

"Earl the Pearl," she said to Daddy, "I've got a great opportunity to offer you."

"No," Daddy said.

"You haven't heard it yet."

"I don't trust you and your opportunities. Last time you used that line on me, I ended up umpiring peewee slow-pitch tournaments all summer."

"No," Aunt Gretchen said, "this is nothing like that. See, our bowling team just got bad news. Lily Obermeyer is having carpal-tunnel surgery next week, and she's going to be out of commission for six to eight weeks, right through our regionals for the state tournament."

"Uh-huh," Daddy said with deepening suspicion. "And you want me to bowl in her place."

I couldn't hear anything, but she must have grinned at him.

"Oh no," Daddy said. "You've got a sub on your team, haven't you? Isn't Harold Jannsen your sub? Use him. That's what subs are for."

"We can't count on him this time of year. He does custom corn picking at night, so he's out of it all through November and into December, depending on weather conditions. No, Early Bird, my dear darling favorite brother-in-law, we have to have someone we can depend on. I know you used to bowl before you and Vesta got married, and I know you were well up in state tournament play. You are the one I want. Come on, Early, be a sport."

"Not by the hair on your chinny chin chin. Just drop the subject."

I'd never heard Aunt Gretchen whine or beg for anything before. She'd never had to, being built like a bulldozer, with a personality to match. It was fascinating to hear her going at it with the sweet talk and pleading. It didn't do any good, but it sure proved how much she wanted Daddy to bowl on her team.

And of course, to a steel-trap mind like mine, a wink is as good as a nod. I read that in a book someplace and I never did know what it meant, but somehow it seemed to fit the occasion now.

I winked and nodded myself into bed, ignoring

GeorgeAnn's act. Her half of the room was across the chalk line from my half, and there's no way I could help turning on the light in both halves so I could see to get undressed. Of course it woke her up and she went through her usual routine of groaning and kicking her legs around in the blankets to show how mad she was.

I didn't care. Life was wonderful. I was going to get James.

All I had to do was make a deal with Aunt Gretchen. That shouldn't be hard. When I promised to deliver Daddy to her bowling team, she would be more than happy to pay off by going out with Edgar. And being a witch of honor, he of course would pay off by putting a spell, or whatever, on James, who would fall instantly in love with me.

Unless the spell misfired and shorted out the lights in the gym, or lowered the prices on school lunches.

But I supposed those were the chances you took when you dealt with the Powers of Darkness.

The next day after school I told the bus driver I had a ride home, then took the long walk out to the edge of town. There was a turquoise metal building along the highway, with a sign in the shape of a smiling car: the Happy Auto Body Shop.

I went in, past the display shelves of fan belts and oil-change wrenches and felt-skunk car fresheners. There was a high knotty-pine counter with two men leaning over it, leafing silently through a parts catalog.

"Hi, Roach. Hi, Pat," I said as I went around behind the counter.

The fat guy, Roach, was Aunt Gretchen's boss. Pat was his son-in-law, whom he couldn't stand but had to hire anyway to keep his daughter happy. It cheered me to be reminded of what a loving father will do for his daughter. I was going to need that pretty soon.

Aunt Gretchen was in the little back office, hunched over a gray metal desk, posting figures in a ledger book while she watched a soap opera on a little TV.

"Hey, Hair," she said when she saw me. "What brings you out of the woodwork?"

"I wanted to talk to you, oh favorite aunt of mine."

"Uh-oh. That sounds like a touch. What do you need? money? something to drink?" She heaved herself out of the chair and went over to a battered pop machine. Two punches to its left flank and a hard kick just under the coin-return slot, and it gave up. It clanked out a can of nice cold pop and kind of sighed, as though it were glad its daily beating was over with.

Aunt Gretchen pitched me the can with a nice controlled underhand toss, and we both sat down. She even turned down the volume on her story. But as soon as she did that, Roach stuck his head around the door and said, "Turn it up. I was listening."

We had to go out and sit on the old car seat along the wall in the shop so we could talk in private. The phone rang. "Get that, Roachie," Aunt Gretchen bellowed, and settled herself sideways on the car seat to give me her full attention.

"I need a favor," I said. "You remember that guy I was talking to last night at bowling?"

She snorted. "Edgar the wimp, you mean? Edgar the insect? Edgar the mealworm? Edgar the . . ."

"Uh, yes, that's the one. Edgar Temple. He was very nice, I thought."

She reared back and looked at me. "Oh, come on, Dagmar. He's a freak of nature." She belched and thumped herself on the chest with her fist.

"He's in love with you," I told her. "You shouldn't make fun of him. He wants you to bear his children."

The acoustics in an auto-body shop are very good for echoing bellows of laughter. I didn't think they were ever going to stop.

"All he wants is a date with you, Aunt Gretchen. Just so you can have a chance to get to know him. Please, pretty please go out with him."

"Never in hell. Never under any circumstances. Never never never. There is not enough money ever printed in this country to bribe me into going out with that slug."

With a deep breath, I fired off my best shot. "If I get Daddy to bowl on your team for you, will you go out with Edgar?"

She stared at me for a very long time. "Yes," she said.

I collapsed in a huge sigh of relief. James was as good as mine.

Aunt Gretchen said, "Dagmar, what's it to you whether I go out with him or not? What skin is it off your nose?"

I was tempted to tell her but stopped myself in time. If Edgar wanted her to know about his being a witch, that should be up to him to tell her. It could easily be the kind of thing that would put another person off, on a first date especially.

So I played it cagey. "I just like him, and I love you, and I want you both to be happy."

"And you think a date is going to do that?"

"Just give him a fair chance, will you, Aunt Gretchen? He's such a nice guy, and he's crazy about you."

"Well," she said thoughtfully, "I have to admit that doesn't happen too often in my life. Not since that mealworm of an ex-husband of mine ran off with the dispatcher from his trucking company even though she had four kids under school age."

"But you used to beat him up, didn't you?"

"Only a little bit," she said defensively. "Only once in a while, when he really bugged me."

I had a sudden moment of uneasiness. I sure hoped Edgar knew what he was letting himself in for.

"Oh," I said, "can you drive me home after you get off? I missed my bus."

"I reckon."

We went back to her office and she booted Roach out so I could have the chair to watch soaps in till quitting time.

Every one of those love scenes on the seven-inch screen starred me and James.

Five

When Aunt Gretchen dumped me off at home she said, "Okay, now, we've got a deal. I go out with your friend the mealworm the minute your dad agrees to bowl, and remember, we need him by next Wednesday night."

Piece of cake, I told myself, waltzing into the house in a swirl of hair. Everybody was moving in a slow wave toward the dining room. Mom bellowed, "Chow time, come and get it or I'll throw it to the hogs." We don't have hogs, that's just her old joke.

I gave my sweet darling daddy a big smoochy hug and a kiss on his bald spot as I passed his chair to my own.

"No," he said.

"No what?" I answered sweetly. "I haven't asked you for anything, cutesy-pop."

He gave me a dark look and said, "You're in stage one of asking me for something, cutesy-kid. I'm not that easy to get around."

Yes he was, but I didn't argue, I just passed him the meatloaf and held the dish while he took his slice.

After supper, while Cootie and I helped clear the table, David and Deaney played wheelbarrow with Delight, holding up her legs and walking her on her hands and making her laugh herself silly. Daddy sat at the table and smoked and looked like a happy man despite the fact that GeorgeAnn was practicing "Twinkling Stars" on the piano right beside his ear.

As usual, she started off soft and nice, but kept getting louder and louder with every repeat. And if you ask me, "Twinkling Stars" isn't the kind of song you can do that to and still have it sound like anything. But I gritted my teeth and endured. I was going to need all of Daddy's goodwill pretty soon.

Finally Daddy yelled over the noise, "Thank you, GeorgeAnn, you've delighted us long enough," and shut the keyboard cover fast. She got her fingers out in time. She always does.

As soon as I could get out of the kitchen I followed Daddy to where he was just sinking down into his big chair to watch television. I sat on his lap and tickled the fuzzies in his ear. That drives him nuts.

"Okay, Dagmar," he said, slapping my hand away from his ear. "Just come out with it and tell me what you want. During the commercials."

I sat incredibly quietly with my head under his chin till the commercials came on. Then I went into action. I had three minutes, tops, to win James.

"Daddy, Aunt Gretchen really wants you to bowl on her team. She really needs you. Just for a while, till what's her name gets over her wrist surgery. Please? For me, your firstborn child?"

He pulled back to where he could look me in the eye. "Bowl on Gretchen's team? What's that got to do with you? What are you after?"

I don't usually lie to him, because for one thing he can see right through my brain. But these were desperate times. He might understand my wanting James Mann for a boyfriend. After all, he was the heir to one of the best dairy setups in the county. But no way would he ever believe Edgar was a witch or that the Powers of Darkness were going to soften James up with a spell.

I got inside my hair and snuggled under his chin again, where he couldn't see what I was thinking.

"I just want everybody to be happy," I said in my little sweet voice. "I love Aunt Gretchen, and she won't be happy till you say you'll help her out. And you know you used to love to bowl, so you'd be happy if you started bowling again. So why don't you?"

"I just won't. Period. Forget it."

31

"But why?"

Sometimes if sweetness won't work, whining will wear him down. I can whine with the best of them. Well, I'm not as good as GeorgeAnn. Her whine will absolutely set your teeth on edge.

"None of your business. I'm just not going to, so get off the subject—and my leg. It's going to sleep."

The commercials were over by that time, and I wasn't getting anywhere, so I wandered to the back bedroom and watched Mom stuff Delight into her jammies. Mom is a baby-nut. She kind of loses interest in her kids after they quit being babies. Well, she doesn't lose interest; I don't mean that. She still loves us and bosses us around, but whoever is currently the baby, that one is her real hobby.

"Mom," I said, flopping across the bed, "how come Daddy doesn't ever bowl anymore? He used to be good at it, didn't he?"

"Your daddy was one of the top men bowlers in northeast Iowa. He had a lovely follow-through, I remember. Fact of the matter is, that's how I fell in love with him."

"Huh?"

Delight, realizing she was headed for her crib, started yelling and windmilling with her arms and legs. Mom put her down anyhow, then opened her jammies, put her mouth down on Delight's belly, and blew against it till it made foghorn sounds. Delight got to laughing and pulling Mom's hair. I didn't think I was ever going to get Mom's attention back onto important things, but finally she gave Delight her stuffed dinosaur and sat down across the bed from me. Mom is very heavy. I had to hang on to keep from rolling downhill onto her.

I said, "Did you really fall in love with Daddy because of how he bowled?"

She laughed so hard that all her chins bounced. "That was just the first thing I fell in love with. Me and my girlfriends used to hang out at the bowling alley, you know, watching the boys."

I felt close to her just then, like she's already felt and done everything I feel and do and she's come through it okay. That was a good feeling!

"Earl Schultz was a lot older than I was," she went on. "At first I never noticed him much. I figured he was an old guy; married, probably. And I was looking at the boys I knew from school, making eyes at them. But one night I went over to where your daddy was bowling with some team he was on and I watched him. He had a kind of a . . . tender way of holding the ball. He'd sort of pet it, smooth it with his hands before he bowled, and I could see a lot of kindness and gentleness in that, just the way he did that, you know. And he was almost like a dancer the way he'd run into the release. After the ball left him he'd hold that pose, one leg crossed over behind him, his hand up in the air like the Statue of Liberty, with his fingers still so graceful. He never moved a muscle till the ball was home safe."

"And that made you fall in love with him?"

She reached over and hooked my hair behind my ear like she always does. "No, but sometimes a woman can tell a lot about a man by little things so subtle she doesn't even know it herself, consciously. They call it women's intuition, but I think all it is is noticing tiny details subconsciously. Like the way your daddy gentled that bowling ball and gave it his whole attention, kind of lovingly. I could just tell he'd hold a baby the same way. Not that he'd pitch a baby down a bowling lane."

She grinned, and I picked up on the joke.

"It'd be so hard to get your thumb out of its belly button when you let go of it," I said, looking serious.

"Yes, and it might bite you. You don't have that problem with a bowling ball."

"On the other hand," I said, raising a finger wisely, "you could train it to stick out its arms and legs when it got to the pins, and you'd have a strike every time."

"You'd have a pretty funny-looking baby, too, by the time you'd bowled it in a few tournaments."

When we were through laughing, I said, "But why did Daddy quit bowling? Why won't he pinch-hit for Aunt Gretchen when she needs him so much?"

Mom got up off the bed, turned out the light, and motioned me after her.

"He has his reasons, and they're none of your business." She was whispering by then, because Delight was asleep, but her message was loud and clear. Leave your daddy alone, quit bugging him about bowling.

I got the message. But I wasn't ready to give up yet. Not with James as the prize at the end of the battle.

If ear tickling and whining and pumping Mom wasn't going to work, I'd just have to go on to Plan B. As soon as I figured out what it was.

Six

All the next day, which was Friday, I kept up the smoochy sweet stuff whenever Daddy was within range. I didn't whine or beg. Occasionally I mentioned bowling, just casually. Like patting him on his little beer belly and saying how much slimmer he used to be back when he was bowling all the time. Subtle things like that.

Saturday he had a job hauling a load of hogs for a guy. Sometimes I go along on jobs like that, but this time he didn't ask me. My daddy has several jobs. He works for the city of New Berlin: drives the town snowplow in winter, mows along the highway and around the cemetery in the summer, cuts down dead trees that might fall on people's roofs, stuff like that. And he does other jobs when people need them, like driving stock trucks for the local livestock buyer if he needs extra help, or helping his buddy Denny at the town's one gas station when Denny goes out running traplines or ice fishing.

Lots of times he takes me with him. When he mows along the highway I can ride along and collect pop cans and keep the refund money from them. And at Christmas he always lets me hand him the strings of lights as he hangs them along Main Street and crisscrosses them over the intersection by the stop sign.

I wasn't crazy about delivering a truckload of squealing, smelly hogs to their deaths, but I'd have liked to have gone along for the ride. If he'd asked me.

Instead, I figured it was time for Plan B. I put on my best sweatshirt, a green one that makes my hair look almost reddish, and I headed out of town on the gravel-pit road, toward Uncle Dean's. And, of course, past James's house, but I couldn't help that. Walking from my house to my uncle's, you have to walk past James's, and I had a perfect right to go out to my uncle's. That didn't mean I was chasing James. In case anyone was looking, I even walked on the opposite side of the road, past the Manns', so they'd know I wasn't walking past their house on purpose.

I didn't see anybody around the yard. Their dog ran out and barked at me, and I stopped and talked to him for a while, watching through my hair to see if anybody was looking out a window. Nobody was.

Feeling depressed, I went on up the road toward Uncle Dean's. It was another beautiful October day—clear blue sky, rich-smelling hayfields, trees in distant woods just going red on their east sides. I could hear chain saws from at least two directions, people working up firewood for the winter. I'd have been happy at that moment if I hadn't been in love.

Aunt Dorothy and my hippy cousin Neese were both busy in the beauty shop putting blue and purple rinses on old ladies' hair. There was bingo at the Lutheran church that night. In New Berlin there are eleven—no, twelve—widows looking for husbands, and three old guys dodging them. So the beauty shop is always busy on the day of a bingo party. Those old ladies are really competitive. It's scary sometimes, watching them.

Of course Neese isn't a licensed beautician yet, so she's not supposed to do things to customers; but nobody minds if she gives shampoos and helps the ladies in and out of the chair.

I sat around in there for a while, but it was obvious Aunt Dorothy was too busy to be pumped. I wandered outside and went looking for Uncle Dean.

He was outside the milking parlor, lying on his back under the manure spreader. It's a big thing like a wagon. The manure gets hauled out of the barn on a conveyer-belt thing that goes up way high and dumps onto the manure spreader, and the tractor hauls it out onto the fields and spreads it.

Uncle Dean was hitting at something under the

spreader with a big wrench, holding his face screwed shut so nothing yucky would fall into his mouth or eyes. When he opened his eyes and saw my feet beside his head, he wormed his way out from under and sat up.

"What are you up to today?" he asked.

He's a pretty good guy when he's not poking at me and asking nosy questions about my puberty. He's Daddy's younger brother, bigger and taller than Daddy, but with the same kind of handsome, leathery face. His teeth are real, though.

"Just thought I'd come out and keep you company," I said.

He grunted and started back under, so I stopped him.

"Uncle Dean, why won't Daddy ever go bowling? I know there's a reason, and he won't tell me, and Mom won't tell me. But I bet you know, don't you?"

He took a long sniff up his nose and wiped the sweat off his face onto his shirtsleeve. From the crooked grin he was trying to hold back, I could tell he knew. He knew the secret of why Daddy wouldn't bowl. All I had to do was worm it out of him and then . . . well, and then figure out Plan C.

I sat down on the grass beside him and had a shot at the honest approach. Through the years I've found that this is what works best with Uncle Dean.

"See, the thing of it is, Aunt Gretchen really, *really* needs Daddy to bowl on her mixed team for the next couple of months or until they get beat out

39

in the regionals tournament. Her best bowler, besides herself, of course, has to have some kind of wrist surgery. And the substitute can't be counted on this time of year because he does custom corn picking or something like that."

Uncle Dean was having more and more trouble wiping the smile off his face. "No," he said in a forced serious voice, "I can see why Earl wouldn't much want to bowl, especially in a regionals tournament." With that he spluttered and broke out laughing.

"Come on," I whined, punching him in the arm. "Everybody's in on the joke except me. Come on, Uncle Deaney-Beaney. You have to tell me. I won't tell anybody, I swear to God. Tell."

When he got through laughing, he gave me a long, measuring look, trying to decide if I could keep my mouth shut over a secret. Finally he gave in.

"Okay, but if he finds out I told you, I'm going to rip your tongue out with this crescent wrench, you got that?"

I looked at the wrench and promised.

"Well, it's really not such a big deal. I'd have thought Earl would have gotten over it years ago and seen the humor of it himself, but he never did. What happened was, Earl used to be a really good bowler. Bragged a lot, but he was good. They had a town team going then, a few guys from around New Berlin, and they'd challenge Strawberry Point and Littleport and like that.

"Comes along this one year, must have been the year after your folks got married, and as it happened the New Berlin team got into some kind of statewide tournament. They were all hot that year, but your daddy was the star of the team."

He leaned toward me dramatically, and I leaned toward him.

"The New Berlin Bombers made it to the quarter-finals. Made it to the semifinals. Made it to the finals! Went to Des Moines for the state finals. It was going to be on television and everything. Big deal around here. I remember old Harry Thurman even bought a little television set just so he could watch that tournament, after he'd been saying for years he'd never have one of them things in his house."

"So what happened?" I could hardly stand the suspense.

"What happened was, your daddy got all duded up for his television debut. Barbershop haircut, new shiny blue pants with a brand-new pair of suspenders holding them up. The pants was a little too big, but suspenders were a big fad at that time, and he thought he looked like the cat's dinner. He was kind of a show-off back then, about clothes. Your mama had even bought him some silly undershorts with hearts all over them, and he wore them for luck.

"Well, you guessed it. He'd just thrown a whopper of a strike to tie the game, and when he straightened up after his follow-through, those suspenders broke or came unsnapped or something. Down went the

41

shiny blue pants, and there stood your daddy in front of the whole state, on television, in his purty boxer shorts with them little hearts on them."

Oh, poor Daddy.

"We like to died." Uncle Dean was slapping his leg. "Of course, you don't let a thing like that just die. We had to razz him; boy, we had to razz him. When he came home we'd strung a sign all the way across the intersection on Main Street, where they hang 'Season's Greetings' at Christmas. 'Welcome Home, Shorts,' it said. He was called Shorts around town for a good long time after that."

"And he never bowled again?" I asked.

"He never bowled again." Uncle Dean's voice was properly sad, but that wicked smile was fighting its way back onto his face.

I wandered home, thinking. Now I had the secret. What was I going to do with it?

Seven

When Daddy asked after supper, "Who wants to go play bingo?" I threw in my "Me" yell. I was beginning to hatch Plan C, and the bingo party could be just what I needed.

We all crowded into the truck, me up front with Mom and Daddy and Delight, the other kids riding in back on chunks of a dead elm Daddy was working up for firewood. First we went out by Uncle Dean's and dropped off the baby and her bag of diapers and junk. Aunt Dorothy was always too tired to go on bingo nights, after all the shampoos and sets she'd done on all the old ladies chasing those three poor old men.

Everything was all set up in the basement of the church. There was a pretty good crowd, quite a few from town and at least twelve pickups' worth from out in the country. They had the long tables set in a double row down the big basement room, with white paper rolled out and taped down for tablecloths.

Coats and jackets were dumped in a long pile against the wall, right under the pictures of Jesus that the Sunday school kids had colored. There were quite a few green Jesuses. I wondered if that meant something profound, for instance that little kids knew something no one else did about Jesus, or whether they just had more green than other colors in the Sunday school crayon boxes.

Well, I could worry about that later. For now, I had to get on with my plan. I did wonder for a minute whether I could get into trouble, either with God or with the Powers of Darkness, by trying to pull off Plan C in the basement of the Lutheran church. But then I figured They would understand.

At the end of the room was a big window-counter opening onto the church kitchen. The Rachel Circle was selling coffee and pop and homemade pie to raise money for its Mission Fund. I got some money from Daddy, bought Cokes and chocolate walnut pie for the whole family, and settled down at the table to play.

Cootie had gone outside with some friend of his, probably to play their usual stupid game of getting into people's cars and pretending they were stealing them.

GeorgeAnn was over by the beat-up old piano in

the corner, poking silently at the keys. She was under strict orders from Daddy not to delight the bingo players with "Twinkling Stars" or anything else, but she was managing to look pathetically wistful about it. She'd be back as soon as the playing got started. She always had to have her own card, but then Mom would have to help her watch it. It was her way of getting attention.

David and Deaney were never any bother at bingo. There was a little Sunday school room down at the end, with a whole cupboard of stuff for them to play with.

Floyd Cranbeer came down between the rows of tables, passing out the bingo cards and collecting the money: a quarter per card, all profits to go to the Mission Fund. Floyd was the town postmaster, and he never let you forget that he was a power in the community. He was always calling New Berlin "the community." I don't know why that struck me as funny, but it did. Maybe because Floyd moved here from Waterloo, which is a pretty big city. Daddy says Floyd was just looking for a little puddle to be the biggest frog in.

He'd have been a sizable frog in any puddle, I thought. He was almost as big around as Mom. But I knew better than to make fun of him for that. I knew how much it hurt Mom when people made fatty jokes, and I knew she really couldn't help being fat. It had taken me a while to figure out why she never wanted to go to Parents' Day at school, why she'd always tell Daddy to go on without her, she'd stay home with the baby. It was because she didn't want kids teasing Cootie and GeorgeAnn and me for having a fat mom. You can't make fun of people who love you enough to do that for you.

So I never went along with the other kids when they called Floyd fatty names. But I did think he was kind of silly when he pretended to be such a big shot in "our community" just because he was the postmaster and the bingo master.

He was actually pretty good at the job of bingo master. He had a much stronger, handsomer voice when he called "B-thirteen" than Reverend Krutchlow did when he used to call the games. Floyd was kind of dramatic about it, like a television announcer. And he always picked somebody, usually a little kid, to draw the numbers out of the wire drum that looked like a hamster cage.

As he came down the table selling cards, Daddy slipped me a quarter and I held it up to Floyd. "Give me a good one," I said, as I always did.

"Guaranteed winner," he said, as he always did.

I was getting nervous. My plan was all hatched in my head, and it was simple enough, but it still made me nervous.

The door opened and some more people came in, shed their jackets, grabbed chairs at the end of the table, and bought cards.

Oh, no. It was James Mann and his parents. Rats. Rats and mice and fishhooks, I swore under my breath. Any other Saturday night I'd have been thrilled spitless to be in the same room as James. I'd be figuring out how I could change places and sit closer to him without looking like that was what I was doing.

But not tonight. Rats and double rats.

Floyd cleared his throat and clanked his car keys against the numbers cage. "Are we all set for another night of killer bingo? Let's see, who would like to draw for me tonight?"

Of course, you guessed it, GeorgeAnn was right there under his elbow, grinning up at him like a congenital idiot.

"GeorgeAnn Schultz? Would you like to be our games mistress for the night?"

Stupid question, Floyd. Anything that involves showing off, you know GeorgeAnn is going to be right there. I asked Mom once if she was absolutely positive GeorgeAnn is my sister. She was.

We all had our little plastic disks piled in front of us. I grabbed a handful and waited for the first number.

GeorgeAnn fished and handed, Floyd baritoned it out over our community. "I-eighteen."

"You are not," called some wiseacre from down the table.

A few people covered I-eighteens on their cards. Not me.

Should I do it on the first game? I wondered. Nah, why spoil the whole evening.

47

The first game went fast. I only had three numbers covered, counting the free square, when Mrs. Mann sang out, "Bingo."

She read off the numbers under her markers to prove she really had won, and Floyd checked them against his numbers, just like an Important Person in the Community would do. When everything checked out, Mrs. Mann got her prize, a gift-wrapped box of Duncan Hines devil's food cake mix.

A few people had to call out jokes about giving devil's food cake mix in the church basement. Then we went on to the second game, some people keeping their cards, others deciding to try new ones. Mom had four cards going at once. Bingo was about her best sport, and she played it on a professional level. Two was all Daddy ever tried to do at once.

The next game started. I got tensed up, thinking maybe I'd do my thing this time. But I lost my nerve and an old guy across the table from me won. He was one of the three bachelors, so of course about five of Aunt Dorothy's frizzy blue hairdos popped up and started making a fuss over the guy, teasing him about his prize. It was a bar of Dove facial soap.

"Okay, now," I told myself. "This is it."

The Powers of Darkness may have been helping me. Almost right away I got G-fifty, G-forty-six, and G-fifty-eight.

I got all tense.

Floyd called, "G-fifty-one."

I didn't have it. But I jumped up and yelled, "Bingo."

Daddy started looking sideways at my card, so I snatched it up where he couldn't see it, and stood there grinning on the outside. On the inside I was wincing and cringing because I was having to make a total fool of myself in front of James. My heart cried out, "I'm doing this for you," but of course I couldn't say it out loud.

Floyd said, "Okay, Miss Dagmar, read off your numbers."

Here it came.

"G-fifty," I called.

"Right," he answered.

"G-forty-six."

"Right."

"G-fifty-eight."

"Right."

A long, pregnant pause. I got red all over and looked down at my card. In my humblest voice I said, "Oh. I guess that's all I have."

Floyd looked down on me from his great height as games master and power in the community. "Dagmar," he said, "that's only three numbers."

"I know it."

"You don't have bingo. You've only got three numbers."

"I know it. Sorry. I made a mistake."

I sat down. There was a rustle of voices through the room, some making fun of me, some relieved that the game wasn't over. I sat there trying to disappear until finally, a million years later, the night was over at last and we put on our jackets and started home.

Now, I thought to myself as we went into the house in a long, sleepy line. Now, to find out if my great sacrifice had paid off.

Eight

Part Two of Plan C went into action first thing the next morning. It was Sunday and we'd had a late night out, so I knew nobody would be up too early, except Delight.

I went downstairs about nine, wearing the prettier bathrobe of the two I own. It's dark red velour with satin trim. I thought I looked very sad and wistful and appealing in the mirror as I brushed my hair and picked the sleep crumbs out of my eyes.

I'd timed it just right. Mom was in the kitchen and the little kids were watching cartoons on the living room floor. And Daddy was still in bed but awake. I started to jump on him and give him my usual morning smooch, but that would have ruined the mood I was trying to set up.

So instead, I just wafted into a sad sitting position on the corner of the bed, where he could see me, and sighed.

He opened one eye. "Is that the angel of death hovering over my bed?"

"Yes." I didn't want to get into a joke thing with him, but I didn't want to overplay it, either, so I just smiled a very small heartbroken smile and waited for him to ask me what was the matter.

His one open eye started rolling back under the lid like he was drifting off to sleep, so I bounced the bed and gave another huge sigh.

With his eyes closed and half of his mouth buried in the pillow, Daddy said, "Okay, Dagmar. What do you want now?"

"I don't want anything," I said, wounded to my core.

"Then why are you drooping and sighing all over my bed at this ungodly hour of the morning?"

"Oh," I said in a faraway voice, "I was just feeling sad. I made such a fool of myself last night at bingo, I'm never going to be able to play bingo again as long as I live. And I loved it so much. I'm really going to miss it."

His top eye popped open and stared at me.

"What are you talking about?"

"You know. When I stood up and yelled bingo when I only had three numbers covered. I made such a fool of myself I could never go to bingo night again."

"Dagmar, you're being stupid."

"No, it's true," I insisted. "Once you make a fool of yourself in public like that, you can't ever face people again. I can see now why you never went bowling after . . ."

I suddenly realized I was in trouble. Open mouth, insert foot, Dagmar.

"After what?" he asked in a level voice.

I couldn't think of any way to explain how I knew about his pants falling down on statewide television, without getting into trouble with Uncle Dean. I knew that loving uncles don't actually rip out nieces' tongues with crescent wrenches, but still . . .

"Somebody told you about my little bowling incident, didn't they?" he asked in an even voice. One eye and half his mouth were still buried in the pillow, so he had to talk funny.

I shrugged. "I guessed it."

He wasn't buying that one for a minute. I couldn't blame him—it was pretty weak.

"So in other words this is your way of trying to con me into bowling on Gretchen's team. You make a horse's tail out of yourself in public and then come moping in here telling me you'll never play bingo again. And then I'm supposed to try to talk you out of it and show you how foolish you are to quit doing something you enjoy just because of one unfortunate incident, right?"

I didn't say anything. God, why bother to try to fool parents?

"And then, after I give you my big argument to get you to keep on playing bingo, you turn that same argument right around and fire it back at me, and I'm supposed to give in and say you're right, I'll go join Gretchen's bowling team. Am I on target here, Dagmar?"

"More or less," I muttered.

His eye closed and his nose went sideways as he burrowed deeper into his pillow. "Okay," he said out of the corner of his mouth.

I looked at him. "Okay what?"

"Okay, it was a dumb trick, and you should know better than to try to outfox old Dad. But if it means so much to you that you'd stand up and yell 'Bingo' with only three stupid numbers on your card, I'll do it. But I will never figure out how your mind works. Your sneakiness didn't come from my side of the family."

I was out of my gourd with excitement for the next three days. I'd look at Shelly and start laughing out loud because she couldn't figure out what I was so happy about. Even though she was my best friend, I didn't have the nerve to tell her what was going on. I had told her about talking to Edgar at the bowling alley and how he had this huge crush on Aunt Gretchen and wanted me to help him get a date with her. But I didn't say anything about the witch part of it. Shelly has been known to be a little cruel, laughing at things I've said in the past when they turned out to be wrong.

For instance, like when we were trying to figure out what a hickey was. All we knew was that sometimes the older girls would show up at school wearing scarves up high around their necks and a lot of makeup blobbed over little round bruises on the sides of their necks. They'd act like they were hiding them, but actually they were showing off. My cousin Neese told me that if you had a hickey, that meant you were going to have a baby. Well, if you can't trust your four-years-older cousin for information about stuff like that, whom can you trust? I told it to Shelly and she just about laughed her teeth out. And of course when we started figuring who had had hickeys as opposed to who had had babies, I could see I'd been had. But Shelly never let me forget it.

I sure as heck wasn't going to tell her I'd made a bargain with a witch who works in the grocery store in Strawberry Point, whose mother changes price tags in K Mart. For one thing, she'd never believe me. For another thing, how could I impress her with getting James Mann as my boyfriend if she knew he'd been tricked into it? And third, if it turned out that Edgar was putting me on and there was no love spell on James, Shelly would absolutely never let me live it down. Daddy's pants falling down on live television would be nothing to what Shelly would do to me. Eighty years from now we'd be sitting at the retirement home in our wheelchairs, and she'd be saying, "Dagmar, remember that time when you thought that guy was a witch?"

So I kept my secrets to myself, but I couldn't help

bursting out with the joy of life every once in a while. I even caught myself grinning at James a couple of times on the bus, after I got past the embarrassment of the bingo incident.

I could hardly wait for Wednesday night. Payoff time!

Nine

The Happy Bodies bowling team marched into battle: Aunt Gretchen, Roachie, Evelyn Klein, and Earl the Pearl Schultz. Everyone wore an electric blue shirt with a picture of a grinning car on the back. Daddy was the only one who wore his with the tail out, and I wondered if that was for protection in case his pants fell off again.

The whole family came along to watch Daddy make his Big Comeback. Mom and Roachie's wife sat at a table right behind the team's bench. They both had babies on their laps; the babies spent most of their time trying to crawl across the table and eat cigarette butts out of the tin ashtray.

GeorgeAnn and Cootie were loose around the place somewhere. I was supposed to be keeping an eye on David and Deaney, but they were easy. Over by the door was a row of game machines. The boys didn't have money to play them, but they pretended to, and they could make as much noise as they wanted. Who could hear them, in here?

So I was free, free, free. Edgar wasn't here yet, so I watched the beginning of the game, but at my own table, three away from Mom. I could see what she meant about Daddy's style. The first couple of turns he took, he was kind of rusty. Got a gutterball once. I held my breath for fear Aunt Gretchen would go back on her word when she found out Daddy had lost his magic touch.

But then he hit his stride and got a spare, then a strike, and after that he was poetry in motion. He'd caress the ball and have silent communion with it, then stand real still, then *deliver*. He'd hold his curvy one-footed pose like a statue in a garden, hand in the air, fingers out in ball-hole position, till he heard the crack and clatter of ten wooden pins getting knocked galley-west. He was beautiful.

I could tell Mom was falling in love with him all over again, too, just from the look on her face. I had to yell, "Mom, Delight," to bring her back to earth in time to pull Delight's fist out of Mrs. Roachie's glass of beer.

Every time the door opened I looked. About halfway through the first game, Edgar finally came in. I was about to go nuts by that time. He saw me and came right over and sat down.

"Where have you been?" I hissed.

"I had to drive Mother over to choir practice," he whispered. "Why are we whispering?"

"I don't know," I whispered back. "But I've got good news for you. Aunt Gretchen will go out with you. Tonight. After the game, if you don't mind sweat, she said."

His whole little colorless face just lit up like a sunrise. I thought his eyes even got a little misty, but his glasses were so thick I couldn't be sure.

"You did it. Dagmar, you're wonderful."

You don't know the half of it, I thought.

"How did you pull it off?" he asked. "No. Wait. Don't tell me that. I don't want to know. All I wanted was a chance to let her get to know me, and you did that for me. If there's anything I can ever do for you, rump steak at wholesale price, anything at all. I'll special order caviar for you. No, I can't do that, that's out of my department. Rock Cornish game hens. Do you like—"

"Oh, whoa," I said, talking out loud for the first time. "What is this 'anything I can do for you' routine? We had a deal, remember? I get you a date with Aunt Gretchen, and you put a love spell on James Mann and make him my boyfriend. Don't you try to weasel out of it, either. I don't care what evil powers you have, I'm not standing still for a double cross from anybody. You don't know what I had to do to—"

He grabbed my wrist to shut me up. People were

looking at us, Mom especially. I gave her a wave and a big toothy grin to show her I wasn't being kidnapped or anything. She went back to watching Daddy and Delight.

"You're right," Edgar said. "I didn't really forget. I just got so excited there for a minute, it blew my mind."

Wouldn't take much of a wind to do that, I thought. Witch or no witch, this one was no mental giant. On the other hand, what would Aunt Gretchen do with a smart boyfriend?

I said, "So you are going to do the spell, right?"

"Absolutely."

"When and how?" I demanded.

"When would you like?"

I thought about that. "Tomorrow morning on the school bus. I get on at eight, James gets on about ten minutes after. We're on there together till about ten minutes to nine, so you've got forty minutes to hit him with it."

"No problem," Edgar assured me. He kept looking over toward Aunt Gretchen, trying to catch her eye.

I punched his arm. "Hey, earth to space traveler. Let's finish the business at hand here before you get carried away. How are you going to do it? How will you be able to aim it at him? How will I know when it happens?"

He held up one finger wisely. "Trade secrets, Dagmar. Just leave everything to me. I'll get the job done; let's say eight-fifteen. And you'll know."

I had to be satisfied with that.

When the game was over, I stood up and waved my arms at Aunt Gretchen, and she came over, puffing and sweating and grabbing a beer at the counter on her way. She had a towel slung over her shoulder, and she kept mopping her face with it.

Now, if it had been me on my way to a table to meet a man willing to move heaven and earth for a date with me, I would have gone to the rest room first and washed off, and combed my hair and put on eye shadow and gloss lipstick and shot a little stinkum behind my ears and down my neckline. But I guess Aunt Gretchen and I play in different leagues in the game of catching guys. I'd do anything. She doesn't even comb her hair.

Of course, she never catches any guys, either.

Except Edgar, and from the look on his face when she thumped down beside us, Aunt Gretchen could have been the Queen of the May, as Mom is always saying. "Who do you think you are, Dagmar, the Queen of the May? Get out of that bathroom right now."

Edgar stood up as Aunt Gretchen sat down. Me being the polite person I am, I said, "Aunt Gretchen, have you met Edgar Temple? Edgar Temple, Aunt Gretchen."

As he sat down I could see his hands were shaking. Aunt Gretchen looked him up and down a time or two, an experience that could make your hands shake if they weren't already.

61

"So," she said. "You're the guy who wants me to have his babies, right?"

Oh God, I thought.

"Not right away," Edgar said with a surprising amount of smoothness. "I thought we'd start off with a late dinner if you'd like, then a few months of dating, getting to know each other, you know. Maybe an engagement ring for Christmas, possibly Valentine's Day if Christmas is rushing things too much. A spring wedding. I like spring weddings, don't you?"

"About like dental surgery," she answered back, but I could see a little light of interest coming on behind her eyes.

Edgar leaned forward. Aunt Gretchen leaned forward. They studied each other. Edgar dipped his hand into his pants pocket and waved a fiver at me.

"Dagmar," he said, still talking smooth and even, "run over and get us a couple of Millers, a large popcorn, and whatever you want for yourself. Then go someplace else to eat it."

"Right," I said faintly.

In case you're wondering how a not-quite-thirteen-year-old can buy beer, in a little town like this everybody knows everybody, so you can. The guy at the bar knew I was getting it for Aunt Gretchen and Edgar. He probably wouldn't have sold it to me for myself.

I delivered the goods and the change and took my Coke and potato chips to another table. Deaney came over and whined at me for a while so I picked him up and sat with my chin on the top of his head, watching Aunt Gretchen and Edgar.

I couldn't believe this. They sat with their heads down kind of close to each other, and every once in a while she'd throw her head back and bellow a big laugh out over the room. I couldn't tell for sure if she was laughing at him or with him, but from the grin on his face I guessed things were swinging along.

"I don't believe this," I said out loud. Deaney stirred and kicked my leg, but he was in the process of falling asleep and didn't much care if I talked to myself in his hair.

It was hard to believe a woman could get a man without even eyeliner working on her side. I finally decided there were still some things about love I didn't have figured out.

Then I forgot about them and went off into a daydream of my own. James was coming over to sit by me on the bus, smiling down at me, saying how nice I looked this morning . . .

Ten

While Shelly and I were waiting for the school bus in front of the post office, where it picks up us and Matthew Garms, I pulled her away from Matthew and whispered, "I have to sit alone today on the bus."

"Why?"

"I can't tell you now. It's a secret, but if it works I'll tell you afterward, okay?"

She gave me a dark, suspicious look.

I said, "You could sit with Matthew."

But I knew that wouldn't work. Sitting together on the school bus is just like telling everybody you're going together. People don't casually sit down together on the school bus unless they really mean it. Shelly and Matthew had been an almost-couple a month or so ago, but it didn't work out, and you don't try to revive a thing like that by sitting together on the bus. It's too public.

The bus came and we got on, and I sat in the seat behind Shelly. Mrs. Hansel, the driver, gave me a funny look in her rearview mirror. I could hear her telling Mrs. Meyer at the café, "Shelly and Dagmar must have had another fight. They weren't sitting together on the bus this morning."

Life in a fishbowl. Blub blub.

All the way out the gravel-pit road my stomach got more and more tingly. We pulled up in front of the Manns' mailbox, and James and his little brother Broderick came running out of the house and got on. Broderick was in second grade. I never liked him very much, although I had hopes that when he grew up and became my brother-in-law he wouldn't be so sickening. At least he'd know how to wipe his nose by that time.

James got on first, came halfway down the aisle, and slid into an empty seat about three up from me, on the left side. The boys always sit on the left, girls on the right. We don't have to, we just do.

Broderick sat beside him, by the aisle. I was wishing James had gotten the aisle seat. I really couldn't see him from where I sat. I could see Broderick's arm and shoulder and ear and cheek. Luckily not his nose.

I checked my watch. Eight-twelve. Tick, tick, tick. I thought I was going to get sick, I was so excited. Eight-fourteen.

Eight-fifteen.

The bus gave a little lurch, and the overhead lights flickered. Usually I don't even notice the lights are on, unless it's a dark winter morning, but today I noticed that flicker.

Oh, no, I prayed. Don't blow the electrical system.

There was another flicker, a bigger lurch, as if the bus wasn't hitting on all cylinders. I squeezed my eyes shut and crossed my fingers so hard the bones almost broke.

Then the bus was running fine again. I opened my eyes.

Up ahead, Broderick Mann had turned around to stare at me.

With love in his eyes.

Eleven

I had to wait till Saturday before I could get to Edgar. And I swear on a stack of witches, those were the longest two days of school I have ever spent. Broderick sat with me on the bus. He followed me toward my school building, and Mrs. Hansel had to fish him back. He was waiting for me to get on the bus in the afternoon, and he sat with me again.

Shelly giggled. Heck, the whole bus giggled, pointed, snorted. Kids sang out in snotty voices, "Broderick's got a girlfriend." "Dagmar's got a boyfriend."

James ignored the whole thing.

The worst of it was, the little faucet-nose never said one word to me. He'd just sit there staring up at me with this stupid look on his face. I kept saying,

67

"Broderick, go back over by James." "Broderick, go away." "Broderick, wipe your nose and drop dead, in that order." Nothing got through to him.

Thursday night I called Aunt Gretchen to see what had happened on her date with Edgar. She said nothing much happened. They went out and chugalugged a few after bowling, had a few yuks and chuckles, that was about all. But then she had to hang up and get dressed. Edgar was taking her to Kountry Manor for supper.

That said a lot, right there. Kountry Manor has carpeted floors and real silverware and on Fridays and Saturdays a dance band in the basement. And nobody goes in there in jeans. Daddy and Mom take us all there once a year on their anniversary, and I tell you, it takes half a day to get our family polished up enough to go into that place.

I told Aunt Gretchen to tell Edgar to call me as soon as he could; it was a matter of life and death.

He didn't call that night, or Friday night even, though I passed up a chance to go to the movies in Prairie du Chien with Shelly's family.

By Saturday morning I was good and mad. I took Cootie's bike without even asking him and rode all the way to Strawberry Point, and if you've ever been along Highway 13 in Clayton County, Iowa, you know what a job that is. One huge hill after another, and they all seem to go uphill.

Finally, what was left of me got to Strawberry Point. I parked in front of the grocery store beside the talking Dr Pepper machine. Have you ever seen one of those? You put in your money, and while it's giving you your can of pop, it sings, "I am your talking Dr Pepper machine. Thank you for using me. I think you're keen."

I used to love that machine till I realized it thought everyone was keen. Now I just use it to lean bikes on. There's probably a profound thought in there, somewhere.

I went clear to the back of the store and rang the little bell on the meat counter, behind the butterfly pork chops. Some man who wasn't Edgar looked out from behind the big window at the back.

"Is Edgar Temple back there?" I called.

"He's not working today. He's in the hospital."

My mouth fell open. "What for?"

"Cracked ribs, I think. Anything I can do for you?"

I was already off and pedaling.

The Strawberry Point hospital was only a few blocks from the store. It was a nice, friendly little hospital, all on one floor. I'd been in it a few times but never back into any of the rooms. I wasn't sure they'd let me go through, but the receptionist gave me Edgar's room number and pointed out the hallway.

He was sitting up in bed watching a little television that hung down from the ceiling. I could see bandages all around his chest.

"Hi, Dagmar," he said cheerfully. "Nice of you to come by." The television set went off, even though he hadn't touched the remote control. I was all primed to read him the riot act, but I got deflected.

"How did you do that?" I said, nodding toward the television.

"Oh, that? That's easy. Watch."

Without moving a muscle he turned it back on and ran through all the channels.

"Fine," I said, my nastiness coming back. "You do that real great, Edgar. So how come you can't do a simple love spell and get it right? Huh?"

He looked surprised. "What do you mean? Didn't it work? It felt like it worked, from this end."

"You clunkhead," I yelled. The man in the other bed raised up and glared at me, and two nurses stuck their heads in and shushed me.

"You clunkhead," I whispered. "You hit the wrong brother. You hit Broderick! He's only in second grade!"

"Oh. Sorry," Edgar said. "Sometimes at that distance the aim isn't real accurate."

"Well, get the spell off of Broderick and onto James, will you?" I'd about had it with this guy.

"Uh . . ." He looked uneasy, and made a weak motion toward his bandaged chest.

That made me realize how impolite I was, not to ask about his ribs. "What happened to your ribs?" I asked, half grudging and half curious.

"Cracked three of them."

"Yes, but how?"

He got a little red-faced and mumbled, "Gretchen

got a little carried away. She only meant to pick me up and give me a friendly hug, but . . ."

I sighed all the way down to my toenails.

We were quiet for a minute, then I said, "Okay, look, Edgar. I'm sorry about your ribs. I'm sorry it was my aunt who did it to you. But you've got to get this spell thing straightened out. You really screwed it up, you know that? I'm the joke of the whole school bus."

"Well, gee, Dagmar, I'd like to help you, but I don't think I'll be able to. At least not for four to six weeks, till the ribs heal and I get the bandages off. See, it has to do with physical powers and mental powers being interlocked."

"You can turn your television on and off," I snapped.

"Yes, but that's, what, six, seven feet away. It's the distance that makes the difference. Now, if you could get James and Broderick to come to the hospital . . ."

"Oh, yes. Sure. I have a clear vision of that. 'Say, James, bring your brother and come to the hospital with me so this witch friend of mine can put a spell on you.' Good plan, Edgar."

He shrugged, although it hurt him. "Then you'll just have to wait it out. Spells will usually last one to two weeks—say, ten days, since this one was weakened by the distance I had to send it. A week to ten days. Maybe less."

"Then Broderick will be back to normal?"

"Absolutely. Guaranteed."

"But James still won't be in love with me?"

He tried to shrug again but winced instead. Half of me was tempted to beat him bloody for not getting James for me. The other half just felt sorry for him.

Love wasn't exactly being kind to him, either, was it?

Twelve

I was too tired and brokenhearted to go to bingo that night. I just stayed home and baby-sat and felt sorry for myself. That can be almost fun, for a while, but then it gets boring.

Sunday afternoon I thought I'd go out to Neese's and see if she had any new wisdom about boys and love since the last time I talked to her. I knew she wouldn't, but there was nothing going on around home. Daddy had his nose in a bowlers' catalog, trying to decide what kind of shoes and bag to order and talking about custom-drilled balls.

Out the gravel-pit road, my feet didn't even need steering, they knew the way so well. It was a chilly afternoon, with fat gray and white clouds going fast across the sky. My parka felt good.

James was shooting baskets against the machine shed again. He waved. I slowed down. He dribbled the ball a couple of times and came over toward me.

"Missed you at bingo last night," he said with an almost-straight face.

"Yeah, well, I had other fish to fry."

He gave me a wise look. "I figured you were too embarrassed to come, after what happened last week, yelling bingo when you only had three numbers. How come you did that, anyway? You're usually a good player."

I looked at him, then sadly shook my head. "Don't ask me to explain. You'd never believe it."

Broderick saw me from the house and started out the door toward me.

"Got to go," I said, and took off running.

The farther I ran, the better I felt. Two reasons. One, James had actually given me a compliment. "You're usually a good player," he had said. That sang through my head over and over as I ran leaping up the road.

And the other good thing was, this time—for the first time—I'd walked off and left James instead of him walking off and leaving me. It made me feel like he wanted to talk to me more than I wanted to talk to him.

So maybe he was going to end up my boyfriend after all. Or maybe I'd decide I didn't even want him. Boy, would that feel great!

I boogied all the way up the road to Neese's house.